CW00869285

Mountain Moggy

W. H. G. Kingston

"Mountain Moggy"

By

William H G Kingston

1866

Chapter One.

The succession of mountain ranges, precipitous and rugged, which extend from the shores of the Irish Sea to the boundaries of England, rising tier above tier, and culminating, at different points, in the heights of Snowdon, Cader Idris, and Plinlimmon, gives to wild Wales that romantic beauty for which it is so justly celebrated. That mountain region, too, guarded by the strong arms and undaunted hearts of its heroic sons, formed an impassable bulwark against the advance of barbarian invaders, and remained for many years, while Saxon England was yet pagan, the main refuge of that Christian religion to which Britain owes its present greatness. Yet subsequently, on account of the inaccessible nature of the country, the inhabitants, separated from their more enlightened fellow-subjects, remained for a long period almost as ignorant as their ancestors in the dark ages; and, till of late years, retained many of the grosser superstitions and customs of those times.

A young traveller was climbing the side of one of these mountain ranges facing the ocean, the silvery waters of which could be discerned in the distance, when he observed, far up, a hut. Solitary and cheerless it looked, scarcely to be distinguished from the sombre colouring of the surrounding ground and the rocks and bushes amid which it stood. It was weather-worn and dilapidated, and appeared altogether unfit to be the abode of a human being; indeed, a thin wreath of peat smoke ascending from an aperture in the roof alone made it likely that it was inhabited. Its appearance offered no temptation to the young stranger to turn aside from the path he was pursuing, and he continued his ascent till he gained a rocky pinnacle, from whence he could watch the sun dipping into the ocean; and hence he could look down, on one side, over a confused mass of barren hills and fertile valleys, rocks, and precipices, heights crowned with trees, peaks bare and rugged, and glens with sparkling torrents dashing and foaming amid them; while on the other side, towards the ocean, he saw before him a wide and smiling valley, with a stream meandering through it, and green meadows and groves of trees, from among which a church spire reared its pointed summit; and near it a cheerful village of white-washed cottages and other dwellings of more pretension; and there were sheep feeding, and cattle wending their way slowly homeward, all speaking of peace and security.

"I could not have selected a more lovely spot to spend an evening in, had I been allowed a choice," said the young traveller to himself, as he took his seat on the highest point he could find. "As I cannot find my home, I could not be better off. I thought that I knew perfectly well the place my family have got to, but I am fairly puzzled with the Welsh names. I ought to have kept my brother's letters in which he had clearly written it down. Whether it is Twrog-y-Bwlch, or Llwyd-y-Cynfael, or Dwyryd-y-Ffetiog, I am sure I don't know. I hit the right post-town, of that I am nearly certain. There's a village in the bottom. I might go down and inquire, but then I probably should not find my way back again over the mountain to the inn where I left my traps. I hope that I may hit it off to-morrow. It's very tantalising, and provoking too, to be so near home, and yet not able to find it. It was very stupid to lose the letter. They do say midshipmen are very careless chaps, and that I am no exception to the rule. Well, I have no reason to grumble. I haven't enjoyed such a sight as this for many a day, though it's something like being mast-headed, except with the difference that I may go down when I like. I should enjoy it more if I had a messmate to talk to about it. The air is wonderfully fine up here. It makes me feel inclined to shout out at the top of my voice, 'Rule, Britannia, Britannia rules the waves, And Britons never, never, never will be slaves,' Hurra! That's it. Hurra, boys! 'We'll fight and we'll conquer again and again.'"

Thus the happy young midshipman gave full scope to the exuberance of his spirits, feeling very sure that no one was listening to him. As he ceased, a curiously wild, mournful strain struck his ear, ascending from below him on the west, and forming a strange contrast to the merry notes he had been singing. It was like the noonday song of the joyous lark, as he soars into the blue sky, answered by the midnight croak of the raven as he sits on the old abbey's ivy-covered wall. He listened. It seemed rather like a continued shriek than a song, or the fearful cry of the fabled Banshee as she flits by the family mansion in Ireland, to warn the inmates, as is ignorantly supposed, that one of their number must prepare to quit the world, its pleasures and its sorrows. The young midshipman's mind was, however, too well trained to indulge even for a moment in any such fancies, for he owed his education to a wise, religious, and loving father. Yet he was sorely puzzled at first to account for the wild strains which floated through the air, till he caught sight of the ruined hut he had observed on his way up, and discerned a large rent in the roof, through which he supposed the sounds uttered by its inmate must be ascending. He was too far off to distinguish the words; but that there were words uttered, and probably as strange as the music itself, if music he could call it, he was very certain. Now the strains rose to a high pitch, now they swelled, now decreased into a low moan scarcely audible.

"Some poor mad creature," said the midshipman to himself. "I should think nobody but a mad person would live in such a place as that; in truth, if anybody had to live there, its solitude and its forlorn condition would be enough to drive them out of their senses; it would me, I know; only I should forthwith set to work to make it habitable. To be sure, I shouldn't be worse off than Tom and I were when we were cast away on that coral island in the Pacific, except that there we had summer all the year round and abundance of food of one sort or another. Here it must be terribly cold in winter, and as for food, a person would soon starve if he were compelled to live only on what the hillside produces." The young midshipman had got into the habit of talking to himself, either during his night watches, or, it is just possible, while at the mast-head, at which post of honour, in some ships, the young gentlemen of his rank used to spend a considerable portion of their existence.

The strange singing continued for some time. As he looked down from his rocky height he saw a number of persons coming up the hill, apparently from the village towards the hut. They appeared from their movements to be children. They got close to the hut, and were hid from his sight. Now they seemed to be running away — now they returned, leaping and shouting, so that their shrill young voices reached to where he sat. Suddenly he saw them all running down the hill, just as children run, jumping and pushing against each other, and evidently in high glee. The midshipman was considering that it was time for him to return to his inn for the night, when a loud shriek, which came from the direction of the hut, struck his ear, and he saw a bright light streaming through the aperture in the roof. "Something is the matter," he exclaimed, as jumping from his seat he ran down the mountain towards the hut: "the cottage or its inmate is on fire; I must do my best to put out the flame, at all events."

Chapter Two.

An old woman was the sole occupant of that cheerless hut on the bleak hillside just described. She sat, on that evening, on a low stool before the hearth, on which a few clods of peat, smouldering slowly with some scarcely dry sticks on the top of them, served as an apology for a fire, and threw out the smallest possible heat to warm the shrivelled palms held up ever and anon before it. As she sat, occasionally rocking herself backwards and forwards, she sang, in a voice which sometimes sounded high and shrill, till it rose into almost a shriek, and then again sank down into a long-continued moan. She uttered words often with great rapidity, though even the poor creature herself might scarcely have been able to explain the burden of her song. The gentle breeze, pleasant in the cheerful sunshine, sighed through the rents in the tottering walls, and amid the branches of the solitary, crooked pine-tree, which bent its riven head over the building, its distorted limbs creaking and groaning as they swayed to and fro; while an owl shrieked his twit-to-hoo to the departing sun, as he prepared to go abroad with other creatures of the night in search of prey; and cold grey twilight covered the mountain-side. There still sat the lone old woman, crouching over the mocking fire. Dark and drear was the hovel—floor it had none, save the damp, cold earth—nor was there a chimney or other outlet for the smoke, except a hole which a branch of the ill-favoured pine-tree had made in the roof, in one of his most restless moods. More light came through this hole than through the window, the broken panes of which were stuffed with rags, dry grass, and heather, though not tight enough to prevent the wind from whistling, and the rain, snow, and sleet from driving in upon the wretched inmate. Except where the solitary gleam of cold evening light fell upon the crouching figure of poor Mountain Moggy, all else in the hovel was gloom and obscurity. Little, however, did Moggy heed the weather. Winter or summer, chilling blasts or warm sunshine, the changeful seasons brought no change to her. Her brain was on fire, her heart cold and forlorn, "icy cold, utterly forlorn and deserted," so she says, and all feeling for outward things has long since departed.

The children stoning Moggy's hut.

Why does Moggy start, clasp her bony hands, open wide her almost sightless eyes, and mutter, "Yes, yes—that's it. Forgive us our trespasses as we forgive them that trespass against us. But it's hard, very hard to forgive our foes. Does God find it so hard to forgive me?" Then again she starts off in her wild song.

Once more she is silent, and listens to some noises outside. She seems sorely distressed. Again and again she starts. The noises increase, children's feet and voices are heard around the hut, and—is it possible?—a stone comes whizzing through the glassless window across the darkened space, and a heavy thump announces that it has found a destination; another, and another follows—some come in sideways, and one striking the window bar glances off and reaches the hearth, whence it drives before it a lighted stick which sends out sparks on every side and causes a faint gleam of light in the hitherto gloomy room. Shouts of laughter accompany each stone; but the sun has set, the sonorous bell of the distant church gives notice, too, that evening has arrived. The children's ears catch the sound. "Away, away! Home, home!" they shout, as they run off from the solitary hut. Out of its window at that moment a bright light shone forth, but they did not heed it as they chased each other down the steep mountain-side, crying out, "Good-night, old witch. We'll stone you again, old Polly Forty Rags. If we hear any more of your witcheries we'll make you wish you'd kept out of this country. Good-night, and bad luck to you, Old Mog." Notwithstanding the words they used, there was terror in the voices of most of the children. Some of them shouted, "She's coming after us! The witch is coming after us! She's mounting her broom, and out she'll ride. Run—run—run!" On this the urchins shrieked louder, and ran faster and faster down the slope. One boy, more daring than the rest, and superior in appearance to most of them, lingered behind, and finding a stone remaining in his pocket of those with which he had, like his companions, provided himself to attack the old woman, he turned round once more, and flung it in the direction of the hut, saying, as he did so, "That's my parting gift, old Moggy. Ha, ha! I see the old lady is going to have a feast tonight, for she has lighted up her banqueting-hall. But I would rather not be one of the guests, though." Pleased with what he considered his own wit, he shouted out again, and ran after his idle companions, a prolonged cry which came from the hut hastening his steps, for he was in no degree free from the ignorant superstition of the rest of the urchin troop.

Chapter Three.

A good log was burning brightly on the hearth, and filling with its glowing, cheerful light the dining-room of Dr Morgan, the new rector of the parish, where he with his wife and the younger members of his family were collected. The rector sat in his easy-chair, his book had fallen from his hand, for he was dozing after a hard day's work of physical and mental labour in the abodes of the sick and afflicted of his widely-scattered parish. His wife had a cradle by her side, but she held its usual occupant in her arms, putting it to sleep with a low lullaby, while a group of older children, boys and girls, sat at the table variously occupied. Charles and Anna having some fresh foreign postage-stamps, arranged them in a book according to the different countries from whence they came, and were preparing a short account of each—a plan their father had recommended, so as to give an interest to this otherwise very useless pursuit.

"This must surely be American," said Anna, holding up a stamp. "How like a well-done photograph is the head. Can it be that of Washington?"

On this William, who was engaged professedly in learning his lessons for the next day, looked up. The rest decided that although the stamp was American, as it was the head of a somewhat sour-looking old gentleman it could not be that of the great Washington, but of one of the later Presidents of the United States. The children were talking in an undertone, so as not to disturb their father.

"Old Polly Forty Rags, the witch, came from America," said William. "But it was from some place which the English don't know about; a wild, barren sea-coast, just like the mountain-side up there, where they say that she used to practise her witch tricks on the vessels which came near, and many and many's the one she has sent to the bottom or driven on the rocks."

"How did she practise her witch tricks?" asked Arthur, who did not very clearly understand his brother's meaning.

"How!" exclaimed William. "That's more than I can tell. I'm only repeating what those who know all about the matter say."

"Isn't she a very wicked old woman then?" asked Mabel, with simplicity.

"Wicked? I should think so! as wicked an old hag as you ever heard of," answered William. "It would be a good thing to rid the world of such a monster; but they say she can't be killed; not if she was soused over head and ears in the river or thrown into the fire. That's the nature of witches."

Anna, who was giving the finishing rub to a stamp just put in, heard the last words, and, looking up, inquired with a slight tone of irony in her voice, "What did you say about witches, Willie? Who has been telling you those remarkably wise things about them?"

"Oh, the people about here, and the other fellows at school," answered Willie in a low tone and somewhat hesitating manner, for he was not fond of having to reply to his sister's pointed questions.

"Oh, the people about here," said Anna, repeating his words. "Is it possible they can believe such nonsense?"

Willie did not reply. "Anna wouldn't think it nonsense if she was to see Old Polly Forty Rags," he muttered. After being silent for some time he added, "If ever there was an old witch she is one."

"You said she came from America, Willie. Why, that's where Frank's ship has been to, isn't it?" said Arthur.

"Of course it is," cried Willie, as if a bright thought had occurred to him. "I wonder whether he heard anything of her there? He'll soon be at home, and then he'll tell us."

"If she didn't send his ship on the rocks," remarked Arthur.

"She'd better not have tried to do it, or we'd pay her off for it," said Willie, as if speaking of some heroic purpose.

"But I thought you said that she couldn't be killed; and if she couldn't be killed, she couldn't be hurt, I should think," observed Arthur, who was called the philosopher of the family.

"Well, I don't know: they say witches can't be killed, and that Old Polly Forty Rags has lived hundreds and hundreds of years," said Willie, justly considered the most thoughtless of the family. "Nothing does hurt her either. You can't think what fun it is to hear the stones bounce against her, just as if she was made of straw. If anything could hurt her, I know a big stone I sent in at her window this evening would have given her a cracker she wouldn't forget in a hurry. It's my belief that she didn't care for it more than she would if it had been a pea out of a pea-shooter."

Anna's attention was again drawn to her brother's whispered conversation. "What are you saying about throwing stones?" she asked. "At whom have you been throwing stones?"

"Why at old Mountain Moggy, of course, or Polly Forty Rags as they call her. Who else should I throw at? She's as hard as she is wicked; and they say she has a whole suit of elephant's skin under her rags, and that's one of the reasons the stones don't hurt her."

Anna had been so busy examining some little three-cornered Cape of Good Hope stamps, that she had not till now clearly comprehended what Willie was speaking about.

"You throw stones at Mountain Moggy!" she said in an incredulous tone.

"Of course we do, and awful fun we had this very evening," answered William, boldly. "We heard them go in at the window and thump against the old witch. The clock struck, and we had to run

11

away, or we should have given her more of it. But it was just as well that we were off, for some of the fellows saw her lighting up her house for her witcheries, and there's no doubt but that she'd have sent down some of her imps after us if we hadn't made good use of our legs to get off."

"What do you really mean, Willie?" said Anna, now quite interested. "You cannot tell me that you have been stoning that poor miserable old woman on the mountain?"

"Haven't we though," said Willie, carelessly, crossing his arms on the table and beginning to pore over his book.

"Willie says that she's a wicked black witch, with red eyes and a blue tongue," remarked little Mabel.

"Don't stuff the little ones' heads with such abominable nonsense, Will," said Charles, looking up from his book. "There's nothing I hate to hear so much; it's wrong, and you have no business to do it."

"No, indeed; it's very wrong to tell stories about her, even in fun," remarked Anna.

"Nonsense and stories, indeed!" cried Willie, indignantly. "They are neither one nor the other. If she isn't black she's near it; and I never said she had red eyes and a blue tongue; but if you two were to hear her screech and howl, as I have, you'd confess fast enough that she was a witch." And Willie turned back to his book with the air of an injured person.

Poor boy, he had not had the advantages of his brothers and sisters, though worldly people would have said that his prospects were far better than theirs. They had been carefully trained in the way they should walk from their earliest days by their parents, who, though not possessed of worldly wealth, felt that they might yet give them the richest of heritages. William had not, like the others, been brought up entirely by his parents. His godmother, Miss Ap Reece, had offered to leave him her property, provided she might have entire charge of him, and his parents somewhat hastily consented. By her he had been well fed and well clothed, but not well educated. She was capricious, fond of gossip, and self-indulgent; and continually she would, in order to be rid of him, send him down amongst the servants, who, as her country residence was in a remote village, were more than usually ignorant. There he imbibed many of their prejudices, and learned to believe in many of their superstitions. Meanwhile, happily, the good seed sown in his earlier days was not entirely eradicated, though he and his brothers and sisters always exhibited in their subsequent lives the different systems of cultivation to which they had been subjected. The residence of William with Miss Ap Reece was brought to an abrupt termination by the failure of the County Bank, in which most of her money was placed. Her means were in consequence so straitened that she was obliged to ask Dr Morgan to take William home.

It was soon after this that the conversation took place which we have already recorded.

Mrs Morgan had been too much absorbed with her infant, and a book she occasionally read, to listen to the undertone conversation carried on by the rest of her children. Her husband continued dozing in his chair, but his sleep was soon interrupted, as was the conversation of the young people, by the violent ringing of the hall-door bell. A servant came in directly afterwards to say that the doctor was wanted immediately. Dr Morgan at once left the room, and when William, sent by Mrs Morgan, went out to inquire why he was summoned, it was found that he had quitted the house without leaving any message to say where he had gone. So startled were the younger ones by the sudden noise, that Arthur upset the gum-bottle over the beautiful new stamp-book. The little fellow looked very much alarmed at what he had done, and possibly in some families angry words and blows would have warned him to be more careful for the future; but Charles and Anna had learned that "he that ruleth his spirit is greater than he that taketh a city"; and the constant practice of this principle made it now easy for them to say to their brother, who sat crying and looking very sorrowful, "Never mind, little fellow; we shall soon make it clean." Then warm water had to be procured, and the injured book cleansed, and a few more stamps stuck in, and the rest put away, and scraps and writing materials cleared off the table. Books were then got out, and lessons looked over for the next day. Mrs Morgan left the room for some time to hear the younger children say their prayers, and to see them put to bed. When she re-entered the room, Dr Morgan had not returned. Dr Morgan's prolonged absence did not create any alarm. He was a Doctor of Divinity, but he had also, in his younger days, devoted much time to the study of medicine and surgery, so that he was qualified to become a regular practitioner. However, he had taken orders in the Church of England, but he never regretted the time he had spent in walking the hospitals, for, biding his time, he had now a means of access, which he otherwise might have lacked, to even the most hardened and profligate. Those who would not have called him in as a Christian minister to advise them regarding their souls, were thankful to get him to attend to the ailments of their bodies. Once in a house he never left it without making himself beloved and respected by its inmates, and insuring for himself, and for his glad tidings, a favourable reception. Although he was not looked upon as a popular preacher, it was observed that wherever he went there was a marked change in the religious conduct of the people.

Such was Dr Morgan. His great difficulty was to give that superintendence to the education of his children which he felt they required, without at the same time neglecting the multifarious duties of his position. His parishioners gained what his family lost. But the strict discipline by which he endeavoured to make amends for the want of that constant watchfulness so important in training the youthful mind did not answer the same purpose. Yet after all he could do, he knew that he must fail altogether, had he not gone daily, constantly, to the Throne of Grace for strength and wisdom for himself, and for protection and guidance for those committed to his charge.

Mrs Morgan had returned to the sitting-room; the elder children had put down their books. It was bed-time. They always waited for family prayers. When the Doctor was absent Mrs Morgan or Charles read them, but as he was momentarily expected, his wife and son were unwilling to usurp his office. At length the hall-door bell rang. It was the Doctor. He appeared unusually sad and serious. The family assembled. His voice, generally so firm, trembled as he prayed.

When he rose from his knees, shading his eyes with his hand, he said, after he had given them his blessing —

"Go to bed immediately, and be up betimes, for I wish you to breakfast an hour earlier than usual, and to accompany me directly afterwards to visit a sick, and I fear a dying person."

The younger children would all have been well pleased at this invitation, had it not been for their father's very grave manner; yet no one ventured to ask him the cause of this, and it was, perhaps, not without a slight misgiving that some of the party laid their heads on their pillows that night.

Chapter Four.

Dr Morgan gave no explanation of what had occurred till Charles and Anna had left the room. He then called his anxious and ever helpful wife to his side. "I much want your assistance, dearest Maria," he said in a tone which showed the depressed state of his feelings; "I was summoned just now to visit a person in a most melancholy condition. You have heard of the forlorn old creature— Moggy, she is called by the country people—who lives in that wretched hovel we can see high up on the side of the mountain. She has been dreadfully burnt."

The Doctor's wife, ever ready with help and sympathy, in spite of the numerous maternal cares to which she had to attend, immediately exclaimed, "Poor old creature! I am sure that she much wants comforts. Shall I not at once send up some sheets and cotton wool? and is there anything else you can think of?"

"The comfort that is wanted, dear Maria, is nearer home," answered the Doctor, taking his wife's hand. "I have a sad story to tell you. On reaching Old Moggy's hovel I found her with her hands and feet horribly burnt; so much so, that, should she survive, which I think it possible she may not, she will, I fear, never recover their use. I found that sturdy old Welshwoman, Jenny Davis, watching by her, and tending her with the care of a daughter. After I had dressed the poor creature's burnt limbs, and done all I could to alleviate her sufferings, Jenny told me that when crossing the mountain that evening on her way home, and having nearly reached the bottom, she observed an unusual light streaming out of the window of Old Mountain Moggy's hovel. Believing that the hut must be on fire, she hurried up towards it, though she feared that she should be too late to render any effectual assistance to its half-witted inmate. So indeed she would, had not another person most providentially arrived before her. On looking in at the window as she passed she saw a young gentleman—a tourist, she supposed—kneeling down by the side of the poor creature; his great-coat was off, he having with it extinguished the flames with which he said that he had found her almost surrounded. Happily, from the great number of under-garments she wore, only the outer rags had caught. He had been sitting on a rock above the hovel, and hearing a scream, and seeing a light break forth through a hole in the roof, he ran down, on the chance of something being wrong, and was undoubtedly the means of saving the poor creature from instant destruction. He and Jenny together lifted Moggy on to her straw bed, and in so doing a piece of burnt stick still smouldering fell out from among her clothes. This was evidently what had set her on fire, but how it had come there, was the question. Jenny was loud in her praise of the young gentleman. He was so gentle, and kind, and didn't mind touching the dirty old creature, and helping to place her in an easy position. He took out his purse, and observing that he hadn't much money, he gave her a handful of shillings, as he said, to help to pay the doctor and to buy her some proper food and clothing. Fortunately he saw a boy crossing the mountain, and running after him he gave him a shilling to go and call a doctor. The lad naturally came to me. The young gentleman would not tell Jenny his name, saying, 'names don't signify.' He had to get back to his inn on the other side of the mountain, and as it was growing dark he could wait no longer; but, as Jenny said, ran off as fast as a deer up the steep, singing and jumping as merry as a lark. He told Jenny that, if he could, he would come back to learn how the poor old creature might be getting on, but that he feared he should be living too far off to reach her on foot. This account was, I own, like a gleam of sunshine, though it threw into a yet darker shade the sad account of an act of which I am compelled to tell you. Having dressed Old Moggy's hurts, I observed several stones, some lying on the bed, and others scattered about the floor of the hut. A large one I especially remarked on the hearth, and which I had no doubt had struck the embers of the fire, and been the immediate cause of its bursting into a flame, and igniting the poor creature's clothes. I asked Jenny if she could account for the stones being, as they were, scattered about in every direction; and she then gave me a history of a piece of barbarous cruelty, the result of a thoughtlessness and an amount of ignorance I should scarcely have expected in the actors. Jenny, though in most respects a true Welshwoman, is free from the ignorant superstition which forms so sad an ingredient in the character of the uneducated peasants of these mountain districts, and was grieved when she found that poor Old Moggy had become the victim of the gross superstition of her neighbours, by whom she is reputed to be a witch who has flown across the sea from distant parts for the purpose of taking possession of the wretched hovel on the mountain. 'I do think, sir,' said Jenny, 'if the poor creature had had the power of flying, she'd have flown to a better sort of a place than this poor shed, scarcely fit to shelter a gipsy's donkey from a snow-storm. When once the mind strays away from the truth, it's impossible to say what follies it won't believe. People don't seem to see the foolishness and nonsense of their own stones. If they'd seen her, as I have, in her right mind, they'd know that a friend of the Evil One couldn't talk as she talks; and as for flying, poor old creature! she can scarcely drag one foot after the other,' Jenny Davis is a thoughtful and sensible woman, though her exterior is somewhat rough," observed the Doctor, who was evidently unwilling, sooner than he could, to repeat the story he had heard. He continued, however: "Jenny gave little heed to these foolish stories, till one day one of her boys came from playing on the mountain-side, with a scared look, and almost breathless, saying that the witch had run after him, shrieking out, and uttering the most dreadful threats. On cross-questioning the child, she found that he did not actually see Moggy running after him, but that his companions said she was, while the shrieks and cries were the result of his imagination. She determined, however, to go and see the old woman herself. Being a woman of action, she immediately set off. When she got near the hovel she found a number of boys yelling, hooting, and throwing stones at it. On her demanding why they did so, they said that the old witch was within, and had done them all some mischief. She had stolen the ducks of the mother of one of them, had milked the cows of a second, and a third declared that she had prevented the butter from coming in his mother's churn. One urchin asserted that his father's horse had died in consequence of her incantations, and another, that she had given his younger brother the croup; indeed, every one had some sort of complaint to make, and vehemently declared that they would pay her out. Whilst she was arguing with them the door opened, and Old Moggy appeared, an unattractive figure, bent with age, covered with rags, and her countenance weather-beaten and scared, and expressive of a melancholy, wild, and restless spirit. The boys, on catching a momentary glimpse of her (for she instantly again closed the door), turned round, and scampered down the mountain. Jenny confessed that she at first felt inclined to follow them, but once more the door slowly opened, and the poor creature looked out to ascertain if her tormentors had gone off. Not seeing them she came out, and Jenny heard her in a plaintive voice thanking God for having delivered her from her enemies; then she broke into a low wail, the words she uttered being disconnected and incoherent. She was on her knees, with her hands clasped and her countenance upturned towards heaven. Jenny's heart was more touched than she had expected. Going up to the old woman, she said, 'These bad boys have been teasing you sadly, I fear, Moggy.' A vacant stare was at first the only reply she received, but on repeating her words Moggy seemed to gather their meaning, and answered, 'Ay, sadly, sadly; but ye knows what we have been taught to say by One who loved us, and died for us. "Forgive us our trespasses, as we forgive them that trespass against us." So ye see that I forgive them, and I pray for them. I pray that they may never be poor and helpless as I am, that they may never be so afflicted in mind and body, and that no evil may fall on their heads; and God will hear my prayers just as much as He will the prayers of the great, and wealthy, and learned, and young, and strong, and happy,' Then she suddenly stopped, and began to shriek wildly and wring her hands, moaning out, 'No father, no husband, no child—all, all gone. Oh, my child, my boy, my hope, my pride!' Jenny tried to soothe and comfort her, and after a long time succeeded in leading her back into the hut, where she became more tranquil, but still apparently was unable to give any connected account of herself. Jenny then, from the basket she was carrying to market, gave her some food, for which she looked grateful, but said nothing. After this, by little acts of kindness, Jenny gradually obtained the helpless creature's confidence; and daily, whenever able, went at the same hour to disperse the boys, who after school hours have, it sterns, been in the habit of assembling, for their amusement, to torment her. Jenny had often threatened to complain to the parents of the boys, and, should they not attend to her complaints, to place the whole case before the magistrates. She had complained to several whose children she recognised, but they either took no notice of what she said, or were very angry with her; and she had therefore resolved, the next time she found any boys ill-treating the old woman, to put her threat into execution. 'Yes, sir, and that I must do, even though some be gentlefolks' sons; one be your son, sir, and sorry I have to speak it. It's that young Master William of yours, and he is the most daring and outrageous of the lot,' she added. 'It's a shame, sir, I'm sure you'll allow, that they should go on so; for a more harmless sorrow-stricken soul I have never met in my life than poor Old Moggy here. All she's gone through would make a book, and it's not to be wondered at that with all her trials, and care, and the cruelty she meets, she is often crazy like. Maybe she's listening now, and knows what I say, for at times she has got as much sense as any one; and it's then that she feels her loneliness, and poverty, and wretchedness, and that makes her go off again as bad as ever, so it seems to me, sir.' I would not at first believe the truth of the accusation brought against William, but on closely questioning Jenny, I found that, without doubt, it is unfortunately the fact that one of our children is capable of thus cruelly ill-treating one of his fellow-creatures; and that he is so ignorant as not to be aware of his crime; indeed he has a vague idea that he was rather performing a meritorious act."

After sitting silent for some time, and grieving over the delinquencies of her son, Mrs Morgan, like a tender mother, endeavoured to find some excuse for his conduct; for one of the hardest trials which parents—who have learned to look upon sin in its true light—have to bear, is to discover that any one of their children is guilty of a crime. The Doctor, however, upright himself, and having a clear and distinct view of right and wrong, would not allow himself to find any excuses for the crime, though anxious as his wife for the good of the criminal; nor did he fail to blame himself, as Mrs Morgan blamed herself, for allowing their child, during the most impressible years of his life, to go from under their charge.

"Still," argued the Doctor, "William has been told what is right and wrong; he has read the Scriptures. He has infringed one of the chief commandments in a most cruel and cowardly manner. I must not be indulgent towards a crime which, if his victim dies, the legal authority of his country will pronounce to be manslaughter. I will endeavour, however, first to ascertain how far he is sensible of his fault by showing him its consequence. Should he give no proof of penitence I must resort to severer measures. I purpose to take all the children with me to-morrow morning to Old Moggy's hut, and I trust that the sight William will there witness will prove, as it must if his heart is not hardened, a sufficient punishment for his act."

"I hope and pray it may," said Mrs Morgan. "I fear, though, that Miss Ap Reece was most injudicious in her management of him, and that he has now been allowed a long course of self-indulgence; and I believe that nothing more effectually hardens the heart and makes it indifferent to the feelings of others, to their sorrows and physical sufferings, than such a mode of treatment."

Long did the Doctor and his wife talk over the subject, and then kneeling, they earnestly placed the matter before the Throne of Grace, seeking from thence guidance and strength. How little, in many instances, are prosperous, healthy, happy children aware that the chief cause of their prosperity, health, and happiness, is to be found in the earnest, trustful prayers of God-fearing parents. Unhappy the children who have not praying parents! thrice blessed those who have, and who, at the same time, set high value on their parents' prayers, and learn betimes to pray aright, and to pray for them as well as for themselves.

Chapter Five.

The sky was bright and blue; a fresh breeze, invigorating and pure, came from the distant sea; the sun, just risen above the mountain tops, shone down with undiminished lustre on the smiling valley, and all nature sparkled with life and light, as the young Morgans, having finished breakfast, assembled at the hall-door to accompany their father on his proposed walk. The elder ones remarked that he looked graver than usual, but hoped that the fresh air and exercise would soon restore his spirits. They all enjoyed a walk with him, for he generally took care to make it interesting, by giving them information on one or more of the various natural objects they met with. There was not a tree, a flower, or a stone, about which he had not something to say which was well worth hearing. Charles called them "Father's peripatetic lectures." This morning, however, the Doctor was unusually silent. His daughter Anna walked by his side, affectionately waiting, in the hopes of an opportunity to bring forward some subject to enliven him. Charles also accompanied him. The rest of the children kept behind, wondering where he was going; Willie especially sauntering at some distance, and thinking that he would rather have been out by himself or with some of the boys with whom he had lately associated. Charles, finding that his father was not inclined to give one of his lectures, bethought him of a subject likely to interest him.

"I say, father, I wonder when Frank will be here. His ship was expected at Plymouth every day. I sent a letter for him to Fox, giving him full directions how he was to find his way here, so that if he could get leave he might come up at once. My only fear is that he may not have any cash for his journey. I begged Fox to advance it, but Frank may not think of asking him. He'll have a great deal to tell us about the Pacific and the coral islands, the Sandwich Islanders, and the other natives, once horrible savages, now mostly Christians. And those people of Fiji—the Black Cannibals of the Pacific as they were called—I want to know if they are as bad as has been represented."

"Yes, your brother Frank will have much to say," remarked the Doctor, and again relapsed into silence.

"I hope he may bring Tom Holman with him. I should like to see the man who saved his life, that I might thank him as he deserves for his bravery," said Anna. "Dear Frank, if it had not been for Holman we might never have seen him again."

"Yes, indeed, I should like to see Holman, the fine and gallant fellow," exclaimed Charles. "The puzzle will be how to get him here. I know that seamen have difficulty in obtaining leave till their ship is paid off, and then there is the expense of the journey. However, I will do my best to manage that."

"And I will help you," said Anna. "I will sell some of my fowls, and the egg money of last year, which I have never spent, and old Mrs Taffety's present, which mamma says I have a right to do just what I like with. Oh, there will be no difficulty about money matters if Frank can get leave for Tom Holman. It will be very nice to see him and to thank him, though it will be difficult to thank him enough."

Dr Morgan had not joined in the conversation of his elder children. He appeared to be absorbed in his own thoughts. Once or twice he glanced round to ascertain if William was following. He continued for some time along the road leading to the village, and then suddenly turned into a path leading up the mountain. William began to feel not very comfortable when he saw this. Still his father might possibly intend to cross over the mountain. He lingered still farther behind, and when he saw him turn off again up the uneven path which led to poor Old Moggy's hut he was strongly inclined to run away.

Surely his father would not wish to go inside the hut. What could he have to say to the old woman? However, go on he must. Fortunately, Charles dropped behind the Doctor, and Anna and William hurried up to him.

"Charley, is papa really going into the witch's den?" he exclaimed in a tone of alarm. "She will be doing him some harm, I am sure."

"Nonsense, Willie," answered Charles. "I did not fancy that a fellow with a head on his shoulders could be such a goose."

"Goose or no goose, I don't wish to fall into the old witch's clutches, nor papa, nor any of us either," muttered William, as Charles walked on again rapidly to catch up their father, and to give a helping hand to the two younger ones. Willie's foolish fears increased when he saw his father walk up to the door of the hut, and still more alarmed did he become when the Doctor, lifting the latch, went in, and then turned round and beckoned to him to enter, though Arthur and Mabel were allowed to remain outside. Most unwillingly he obeyed; but when he got inside the door, not a step farther could he bring himself to advance, and from the furtive glances which he ever and anon cast through the doorway, it was very evident that he would make his escape if he dared. Even Charles and Anna drew back from the pitiable object which met their sight. The light streaming through the window fell on a low pallet, on which, covered with a sheet, lay the form of Mountain Moggy. By her side sat Jenny Davis, whom William recognised as her champion who had threatened him and his companions with condign punishment if they ever again attacked the old woman. Something dreadful was going to happen—William scarcely knew what. A glance his father cast at him made him understand that he must not move. Of course Jenny Davis had told everything. After exchanging a few words with Jenny, the Doctor lifted the sheet from off Moggy's feet.

"William, come here and witness the effects of your cruelty," he said in a stern voice, very unlike that in which he was accustomed to address his children. "Now look at those poor burnt hands. You, and those with you, I have no doubt, caused all the pain this poor woman is now suffering; and should she die, at whose door, think you, will the guilt lie?"

William could not answer. The Doctor, taking out some salves he had brought with him, began to dress the poor creature's limbs.

Anna could not refrain from tears, while she went forward to assist her father and kind Jenny. William stood by without uttering a word, and feeling as he had never felt before.

When the sufferer's hands and feet were once more covered up, the Doctor directed Charles to call in the younger children.

"Listen to what Jenny Davis will tell you," he said, when they were all assembled round the bed.

"Ah, sir, I have a tale to tell which would soften a heart of stone; but I hope none of these young people have hearts of that sort," remarked Jenny, fixing her eyes on William. "She has told me how it all happened, and it may be a warning to that young gentleman never to throw stones at any human being, even though they may be deserted; or, for that matter, at any living creature. They cannot tell where the stone may strike, and what harm it may do. Well, sir, Old Moggy was sitting at her poor fire when those cruel boys came up here again to play off their cowardly tricks. They talk of her imps doing mischief, though they were the imps, and they were doing the mischief, I'm thinking. Stone after stone was thrown in on her. At last one struck the hearth and sent a burning stick under her feet. While she stooped down to remove it, another large one gave her a blow on the head which must have stunned her, for she fell to the ground and her clothes began to burn. The agony she was suffering brought her in some degree to her senses again, when she found herself surrounded by flames, and believed that she was going to be burnt to death. There was nobody near that she knew of to help her, and she couldn't help herself; she knew that, so she prayed for the help of God. Just then the door burst open, and the young gentleman I told you of ran in, and throwing his coat over her, put out the fire. I came in soon after, and helped to put her on the bed. I think that the young gentleman burnt his own hands not a little in tearing off the burning clothes which his coat couldn't cover, but he said it was just nothing, and wouldn't let me look at them even before he went away."

" Listen to what Jenny Davis will tell you," he said, when they were all assembled round the bed.

"What a brave, noble fellow!" exclaimed Charles. "I should like to have made his acquaintance."

"So indeed should I," cried Anna. "Do not you know his name, Jenny?"

"No, my sweet miss, I don't," answered the Welshwoman. "But I think I know where it's written, and that's where the names of the cruel, and selfish, and heartless will never be found."

"God bless him! God bless him!" said a deep voice from the bed.

The children started; it was the voice of Old Moggy. They had not supposed she was listening, much less that she was capable of speaking. The rest of the children remembered William's remarks on the previous evening, and all eyes were turned on him. He stood white as ashes, and trembling in every limb. While they had before been speaking, the window had been darkened by a person passing before it. William had remarked it, and he had taken it into his head that it was that of a person come to carry him off to prison for his misdeeds. The rest had been so interested in what they were hearing that they had not observed that a stranger was near them.

"Ye said that she knows the truth; ay, that she does, and practises what the Word of Truth tells us; for instead of railing she blesses, and from her heart forgives them who have ill-treated her," said Jenny. "Poor, harmless, weary soul that she is! Those young ones who stand there can know little of the sorrows and trials she has been called on to endure. She has seen loss of parents, and property, and husband, and child, and her good name, and all that we think makes life pleasant; and now that she has found her way to this lone place, to die in peace, the Evil One has made these lads come up here to mock and torment her. I mind reading of a good prophet going to a certain village in a foreign land, and the lads came out and mocked him, and called him old bald-head, and what do ye think happened? Why, two she-bears came out of a wood and destroyed forty and two of them. I don't mean to say that Old Moggy is like the old prophet, but yet she is aged and friendless; and those who abuse and ill-treat her are, in the eyes of the Almighty, doing a great wickedness; that they are, I'm sure."

While Jenny was speaking, the lips of the sufferer were seen to move; and in the same deep tones which had before been heard, the words came forth, "but forgive us our trespasses, as we forgive them that trespass against us. Yes, yes: oh, I forgive them; they didn't know any better; they thought I was a witch; they thought I could work charms, and had bad power. Oh! they would not have done as they did if they had known of my weary, weary, aching heart; my poor boy underneath the sea—my husband drowned before my eyes—my sad, sad days, my sleepless nights—my wandering brain—my hunger and thirst—my wretched, wretched life for long, long lonesome years. All these things you did not know of, young gentleman, when you and your companions threw stones at me. Don't think I would curse you for it. No, no. Come near, my children. I bless you, ay! from my heart, all of you. You who ill-treated me and you who never did me harm."

Slowly and reluctantly, with awe in their countenances, the children drew still nearer to the bed. The old woman's voice had dropped through weakness and exhaustion, yet she continued—

"My lot has been very hard, very hard; yet I have had a Friend above who has upheld and comforted me. And yet I have had many trials, many trials, many trials. My brain reels and wanders. I think of my husband and my boy, my only boy, many fathoms deep beneath the cold, cold waves, and then my head turns and my heart changes into stone, and I forget where I am and what has happened."

The old woman began to ramble, and suddenly burst forth in the wild song which she had been singing on the previous evening.

Jenny Davis shook her head, observing, "She'll not be right after this for some time. When the fit comes on her there's no more sense to be looked for till she has had some rest."

"I will send her up a quieting draught and some wholesome food, which will probably do her more good than any medicine," said the Doctor, taking Anna's hand, and motioning the others to move towards the door.

William had hitherto not spoken a word. "Papa, may I take her up the medicine and food?" he said, and big tears rolled down his cheeks.

"Yes, William, you may," was the answer.

Dr Morgan and his children had got outside the hut, and were on their way down the steep side of the mountain, when they heard a cheery shout behind them. Turning round, Anna instantly sprang up the hill, and in another moment was in the arms of a young gentleman who was running down to meet them.

"It is Frank! It is Frank!" burst from the lips of the rest.

"Why, father! Charley! who would have thought it?" cried the young stranger, warmly greeting them; "and Willie, and Mabel, and Arthur! What big people they have become! I little expected to have found you so soon; and you were in that poor old woman's hut, too! Well, that is curious! The truth is, I am lost, or rather I couldn't find you. I mislaid Charley's letter, and though I thought I knew the name of the place, I found, when I got into the country, that I hadn't the slightest notion of what it was; and after wandering about for a couple of days, I determined to write to old Evans, at Bangor, and to await his answer at the inn on the other side of the mountain."

"Then, Frank, you are the young gentleman who saved Old Moggy's life," said Anna. "How delightful!"

"Oh, did I? I merely threw my jacket over the poor creature's legs, and put out the fire which had caught her clothes and would have burnt her," answered the midshipman. "I am very glad I was of use, though it's not a thing to be proud of. It was very fortunate, however, for me, for I don't know how otherwise I should have found you. There is one thing I should like to do, and that is to thrash the heartless young monkeys who threw stones at the poor woman. If I can find them I will."

William looked down, overwhelmed with shame, and almost wished that Frank *would* thrash him.

"Then what brought you back to the hut, my boy?" asked the Doctor.

"Oh, to look after the poor old woman," said Frank, "I understood from the nurse—Jenny Davis she told me was her name—that she has no friends, and so I thought it was but right and proper to come back and see how she was getting on. I dropped a bundle with some old shirts and other things in at the window; but seeing some people there, not dreaming that they were all of you, I of course wouldn't go in. I waited, expecting you soon to go away, and fortunately I made you out, or I should have gone back to my inn, and not known that I had been close to you."

"Bless you, my boy, bless you! may you ever act in the same way from principle, and not merely from the impulse of the heart, good as that may be," said the Doctor, warmly, pressing Frank's hand, and undoubtedly feeling the contrast between his conduct and that of William. "And now let us hear something about yourself," he continued, in a more cheerful tone than he had hitherto been speaking in.

The young sailor had plenty to talk about, though, as he remarked, he found his words apt to block up the hatchway, he was in such a hurry to get them out of the hold.

Charles and Anna were eager to hear about Tom Holman, and William would have liked to hear what his brother was saying, but, in shame, he hung back some way behind the rest, and when they reached the house his father told him to go to his room, and wait there till summoned Frank saw that there was something wrong, but forbore to inquire, hoping soon to have an opportunity of pleading for the culprit.

"Ah, that comes, whatever it is, of his being brought up by old Becky Ap Reece," he thought to himself. "I am heartily glad he is free of her, though he may never get a farthing of her money. He was a plucky little chap, and with good training something might be made of him; but she treated him like one of her poodles, and would soon have made him of no more use in the world than a puppy dog."

Though Frank Morgan was thoughtful, he was one of the merriest fellows under the sun, and among the lightest of heart though not of head. Frank's return brought life and spirit into the house; for Charles, though highly esteemed, was grave and somewhat reserved; Anna was sedate and quiet; and William, since his return home, had been very troublesome, and was looked upon generally as an arrant pickle; while the Doctor and Mrs Morgan were so much occupied that they were unable to think of amusements for their children. Everything, however, was to give way in order to make Frank enjoy his short visit at home; and picnics and several pleasant excursions were planned that he might find the time as pleasant as possible.

Chapter Six.

Dr Morgan loved William fully as much as he did the rest of his children, but he saw that correction was necessary to cure him. Instead of being allowed to welcome Frank with the rest of the family, William was sent to his room, where he remained by himself, not knowing what was next to happen. He was very sorry for what he had done; he had seen the fearful consequences of his cruelty, by which he might have deprived a fellow-creature of life; indeed, he knew not even now whether Old Moggy might not die; and he also saw his own folly in believing that a poor weak old creature, who could not preserve herself from injury, could injure others in the way she was accused of doing, and he wished that he had not thrown stones at her. These thoughts made him very uncomfortable, and he would have been glad to go anywhere, or do anything which would enable him to cast them away from him. It was a great relief when his father came with the medicine and other things for Old Moggy, and told him that he might take them to her, but must return immediately to his room, without stopping to talk to any one.

"Solitude is good for our spiritual welfare, to allow of reflection, but we must not permit it to hinder us in the performance of the active duties of life," observed the Doctor to his wife, when he told her how he purposed treating William. "He wished to take the things to her, and he is the fittest person to do so. It is well that he should feel that he is useful and doing his duty; but at the same time it is necessary that he should understand that the so doing cannot exonerate him from the consequences of his transgressions."

William hastened out of the house with his basket. He knew that if he met any of his school companions they would ask him how long he had turned apothecary's boy, what wages he got, and whether he made the pills as well. He determined not to mind. Still he anxiously looked about, fearing some might appear. He ran on, therefore, till he reached the steep part of the path up the mountain. As he climbed up his heart again failed him, for he began to fear that Jenny Davis would at all events scold him, and that perhaps Moggy, seeing him alone, would say something disagreeable. Still, as he had volunteered to go, it would be arrant cowardice if he turned back. He reached the hut and looked in at the window. Jenny saw him, and saw that he had a basket in his hand.

"Come in, come in, my good young sir," she exclaimed.

The words encouraged William, and he entered.

"It's like your father's son to come and visit the poor and the afflicted," she added. "I'm sure I thank ye, and so does she who lies there, though she's ill able to speak now."

Moggy, whose senses had by this time returned, heard her.

"Ay—bless you, young gentleman! bless you!" she muttered. "I forgive you, and thank you, and am your debtor; and there's One above who'll forgive you if you go to Him."

It surprised and puzzled him that Moggy bore him no ill-will, after all the injury he had inflicted on her. He did not stop to inquire how this was, but, having left the contents of his basket, bent his steps homeward. As he wound his way by the path down the mountain-side, at a far more sedate pace than was his wont, he thought over the matter. Suddenly the words of the Lord's Prayer occurred to him—"Forgive us our trespasses, as we forgive them that trespass against us."

"That's it; she has been very wicked, and so she forgives me that she may be forgiven," he said to himself. "But then I have been very wicked too, and I have nobody to forgive. I don't know anybody who has done me harm; I wish that somebody would, and then I might forgive them." He reached home, and made his way to his room again. No one came near him all day. At dinner-time Anna stole up with a plate of meat and vegetables. She placed it before him, but he felt very little inclination to eat. Anna was about to quit the room; Willie stopped her.

"I know I am very wicked, but I don't know what to do!" he exclaimed, sobbing. "I wish that papa would come and tell me."

Anna reported these words to their father. The Doctor might have hastened at once to Willie, but he judged it wiser to allow the good impression that had been formed to take root. He therefore sent him up the Bible, by Anna, and begged him to read the answer of Paul to the gaoler at Philippi. Anna showed him other texts of Scripture — "Blessed are the merciful, for they shall obtain mercy"; and then pointed out warnings against those who wrong and oppress the poor and the afflicted.

"I know, I know that I have done very wrong, and am very wicked," sobbed William. "Do you think God will pardon me? I do not feel as if I could do anything to make God forgive me, or love me, or be kind to me again."

Anna stopped to collect her thoughts before she spoke; she then said —

"I am very sure that you never can do anything to make God forgive you, dear Willie; and yet I am sure that God *will* forgive you if you seek Him through the Mediator He has given us. God loves to be gracious. If you really are sorry for what you have done, if you repent, not because your fault has brought you into trouble and disgrace, but because you have offended God, then God will assuredly pardon you, for He has promised in His Holy Word to do so. He says 'Knock and it shall be opened to you, seek and ye shall find'; so you see, dear Willie, you may be pardoned if you seek it in the right way."

And she spoke of God's love in sending His blessed Son to save us from our sins, and of the Holy Spirit that He gives us to soften our hard hearts and make them tender, as well as to teach us always what we ought to do.

When she ceased speaking he was sobbing, but not bitterly.

"Pray for me, Anna," said he; "I am not able to pray for myself."

"Oh, be sure all those who love you will pray for you," she answered, kissing him. "Papa and mamma pray for us night and morning, I am certain of that; and it makes me very happy and confident to think so. But still, dear Willie, remember always that we must pray for ourselves."

"Yes, I know, and I will try," said William, as his sister left the room.

The evening approached. Charles brought him up some tea and bread-and-butter, but said nothing. No one else came near him, not even Frank. He thought that Frank might have come, but still he could not complain. How different had been his brother's conduct and his own towards poor Old Moggy! He had thought her a witch, and thrown stones at her, and called her all sorts of bad names; while brave Frank had risked burning himself to save her, and had kindly treated her, and given her money, and come back to see how she was faring.

"And they say that there are no such things as witches, or ugly ghosts wandering about, or such-like creatures," he thought to himself. "I always fancied there were, but papa must be right, and I am sure I hope that there are not. And as God loves us I don't think He would let such things be, to come and frighten us, certainly not to harm or frighten those who love Him. How very, very foolish I have been, to believe all the nonsense I have heard."

With these thoughts, repentant Willie fell asleep. He did not see that his parents entered, when the rest of the family were gone to bed, and bending over him observed how placidly he slept. Then they knelt down together and earnestly prayed for his spiritual welfare. He had sorely felt their absence all day, and was inclined to believe that their love was estranged from him. How far was this from the truth! Thus it is that our Heavenly Father deals with His erring children. He shuts Himself out from them. He allows evil to overtake them, but not the less does He love them. He thus afflicts them that they may more fully feel their dependence on Him, and return like the prodigal to His arms.

Chapter Seven.

Frank had to return to his ship, but after a short cruise he wrote word that he had again got leave to go home; and this time he hoped to be accompanied by his shipmate, the preserver of his life, Tom Holman. The family at the rectory were as eager to see Tom as they were before. Some changes had taken place among them. Willie was very different to what he had been. His masters remarked that he was much improved. From being the most idle, he was now one of the most attentive and obedient of their scholars. His parents, too, believed that they had discovered a real change of heart. His godmother, Miss Becky Ap Reece, had died and left him her heir, her property realising a far larger sum than had been expected; indeed, it was surmised that the poor lady must have lost a considerable portion of her income at cards, or she would have been able to live in better style, or have done more good with it than she had done.

As soon as William heard that cousin Becky's property had been left to him, though of course he was ignorant of its value, he entreated that he might give it to Old Moggy to make her comfortable.

"What, all, Willie? all your fortune?" asked his father, with a feeling of pleasure about his heart.

"O yes, papa, I do not think that I have a right to spend any of it on myself, while she is suffering in consequence of my wickedness," answered Willie, with perfect sincerity.

"I rejoice to hear you say so, my dear boy, but the matter is not left in your power, nor indeed in mine. Until you are of age, the interest of the capital can alone be spent; and I, as your guardian, have authority only to expend it on your proper maintenance and education. It is only, therefore, by denying yourself all luxuries and amusements, and by saving pocket-money, with which I am directed to supply you, that you can help poor Moggy as you desire."

"Oh then, that is what I will do," exclaimed Willie. "Don't give me any pocket-money, or let me have any amusements which cost money. That's almost what I wanted to do; though I should like to set her up as a lady, or in a comfortable house, with a servant to attend on her."

"That would not be wise, Willie," remarked Dr Morgan. "You would expend all your means on one person, giving her more than she requires; and though it would save you trouble, you would be prevented from benefiting others; whereas you should calculate the means at your disposal, and take trouble to ascertain how much good you can possibly do with it. I am also bound to give you your pocket-money, provided I do not find that you make a bad use of it. You must decide how it is to be spent, and of course you are at liberty to return it to me to spend for you."

"Oh, that will do, that will do!" exclaimed Willie, with pleasure in his tone. "But you will help me, papa, in doing what is best with it?"

"I have already anticipated some of your wishes with respect to poor Moggy, and we will see what more can be done to make her comfortable. She says that she prefers Windyside to any other spot on earth, and has no wish to move from it."

On a fine day, when the sun was shining brightly over mountain and moor, and his beams were lighting up the pine-trees and the once dark, ruinous hovel on the hillside, Dr Morgan with most of his children took their way towards Old Moggy's abode. It was greatly changed for the better. A chimney was now to be seen rising above the roof, which had been fresh tiled; there was glass in the window, a latch on the door, which had been repaired, and the lichen-covered walls had been scraped, fresh pointed, and white-washed. When the party got inside they discovered an equally agreeable change. A thick curtain divided the room; a screen kept off the draught when the door was opened; the walls were whitened, and there was a cupboard, and a table and chairs, and several shelves, on which rested some neat crockery. On the inside of the curtain there was a comfortable bed, and some thick matting on the floor. Old Moggy was seated in a large easy-chair, with her feet on the old stool, which before was one of her sole articles of furniture, and good Jenny Davis was making up a nice fire of coals, on which to cook some wholesome meat and vegetables which she had just brought from the market.

"She's getting quite strong and hearty, with the good food and kindness," answered Jenny to the Doctor's question, "How is Moggy to-day?"

"She can talk to ye as clear and sensibly as any one; ay, and there are some glorious things she has been saying to me, which have done my soul a world of good."

"Ay, Doctor Morgan, in one thing Jenny speaks truth. I don't feel the poor demented creature I was a few short months ago," said Moggy; "and it's your tender kindness, and that of your dear boy, Master Willie, and the rest of your children, has brought about the change which ye see in me. I am clothed, and in my right mind; and yet, through the mercy of God, I never, even when my mind was wrong, was cast out from Him. I still sought Him, and found Him. He watched over me and protected me."

"Be assured, Moggy," said the Doctor, "that we are well repaid for what we have done for you. But I must not stay. I came up with my children to-day to see how you were. You require no doctoring, and so I must away. Anna, however, will remain with the rest, as she has brought up a book to read, which may interest you."

When the Doctor had gone Anna took a seat by Moggy's side, and Willie begged Jenny to give him some employment which might be of use.

"There's little enough, my sweet young master, that is fit for you to do," answered Jenny. "There are those few pots and pans to clean, and some cups and saucers, and plates and spoons, and knives and forks, but sure that's not work fit for a young gentleman's hands."

"Oh, any work is fit for me, if it is to serve Moggy," said William, rubbing away at the articles which were placed by his side.

Anna read on in her sweet, low voice. The book contained a true history of one who bore suffering and affliction with patience and perfect resignation to the Divine will for long, long years, till health came back and she enjoyed peace and happiness in this world, and departed full of joy and hope. Moggy, who seemed deeply interested, instantly applied the history to herself.

"That's me, that's me," she muttered. "I have got peace and comfort, and it's a happiness to have all these loving, dear children round me." She paused and sighed deeply, as if a recollection of the past had come suddenly on her, for she added, "But ah, who can bring back the dead—those who lie far, far away in their ocean grave? No joy for me here till I know that I am departing to meet them."

"Dear Moggy," said Anna, interrupting her gently, and fearing that she might give way to her feelings too much, "you have more than once promised that you would give us some of your past history. We should very much like to hear it, provided you do not dwell too long on the more painful portions."

Moggy looked up at her with a sad expression in her eyes.

"Ah, sweet Miss Anna, you do not know what you ask," she answered. "If I were to tell you my history without the sad portions there truly would be little to tell; but I will not therefore deny you. It will do me good, maybe, to know that those I love are acquainted with my griefs, and can pity me, and as it were share them with me."

"We know that you have had sore troubles, and we pity you for them, and we have all learned to love you because you bear them so patiently," said Anna; "therefore if it gives you pain do not talk of your past history."

"Ay, that is kind in you, Miss Anna, to say, but I have the wish now to tell you all; what I have been, and how I came to be as I am," said

Moggy. "Master Willie, ask Master Charles to come in (Charles had returned outside the cottage to botanise), then I'll tell ye all, yes, all. Often and often I've thought of the past, so it does not seem strange to me as it will to you, dear Miss Anna, but ye will not weep for me, for it's long, long since I wept for myself."

A shout from William made Anna run to the door, and from thence she saw Charley shaking hands with their brother Frank, and Willie running down the hill towards them. Another person stood by, who must be, she was certain, Tom Holman. Looking into the cottage again, and crying out, "Frank has come! Frank has come!" she also ran down the hill towards her brothers. There were warm greetings, and smiles, and laughter; and then Frank sang out, "Hillo, Tom, come up here. My brothers and sister want to thank you for enabling me to get back and see them; and tell them how you picked me out of the water and saved my life, and have taken such good care of me ever since."

Tom had, with true politeness, gone some way off out of ear-shot of the brothers and sister when they met. The latter words were addressed to him, and with the activity of a seaman he sprang up the hill towards them. He did not quite come up to the idea Anna had formed of him. Though dressed as a seaman, he was somewhat different to the commonly-received notions of what a British tar is like; still less could he be compared to a refined pirate or dashing rover of romance. He was an ordinary sized, sunburnt, darkish man of middle age, with a somewhat grave expression of countenance. When he spoke, however, a pleasant smile lit up his firm mouth, and his eyes beamed with intelligence. Anna, Charles, and Willie went forward, and putting out their hands one after the other, shook his cordially, and thanked him, in a few simple words, for the manly services he had rendered Frank; each hoping to find means of proving their gratitude in a more substantial way than by words alone. Tom answered them in a pleasant voice, evidently gratified by the way they had treated him.

"Why you see, Miss Morgan and young gentlemen, it was your brother first did me a service, and a very great one too, and so I felt very grateful, and a liking to him, and that made me have my eye oftener on him when there was any danger abroad, and be oftener talking to him; and so, do ye see, all the rest followed in course."

"We never heard of Frank doing anything for you," answered Anna. "We thought that the obligation was all on his side."

"Come, Tom, don't talk about that just now," cried Frank. "I say, Anna, how's Old Moggy? I'm glad to see that you have painted up her abode. I must go up and see her at once, and introduce Tom to her; she'll like to hear about the foreign parts he has been to."

Saying this, he ran up the hill towards the hut. The rest of the party followed more slowly. Tom remained outside; the young Morgans entered. They found Frank seated opposite to Moggy, talking away to her, and telling her how happy he was to see her so comfortable. The poor old woman was much gratified with the attention paid her.

"But where is Tom?" cried Frank. "Willie, tell him to come in. I want to introduce him to Moggy. He will be interested in her, for a kinder heart than his does not beat in the bosom of any man, woman, or child that I know of."

Tom soon made his appearance, doffing his tarpauling as he entered, and taking a seat to which Frank pointed, nearly opposite Moggy.

For a minute or more after Tom had taken his seat Moggy was silent, when bending forward, and shrouding her grey eyebrows with her withered hand, with unexpected suddenness she said, in a deep, low voice, and a strange inquiring expression in her countenance—

"Who are you, and where do you come from?"

"A seaman, mother," answered Tom, "and shipmate for many a year with young Mister Morgan here."

The old woman scarcely seemed to understand what was said, but kept muttering to herself, and intently gazing at Tom.

"Come, Moggy, you'll stare my shipmate out of countenance, for he's a bashful man, though a brave one," cried Frank, who fancied that his friend did not like the scrutiny he was undergoing. Frank produced the effect he wished, and Moggy at once resumed the placid manner she had of late exhibited.

"Your pardon, sir; strange fancies come over me at times, though it's seldom now I get as bad as I used to be," said Moggy. "I forgot how time passes, ay, and what changes time works, but I will not trouble you with my wild fancies. Your honoured father has shown me how I may put them to flight by prayer, by looking to Him who died for us, and then all becomes peace, and joy, and contentment."

"Moggy was just going to give me an account of her early days when you arrived," said Anna.

"I shall like very much to hear all about her, if Moggy will put off her history till another day," remarked Frank. "I promised to return home again without delay, so we must not remain any longer."

"Remember, children dear, time is in God's hand, not ours. We propose, but He disposes as He knows best. He may think fit to let me live, to enjoy the comforts you have provided for me in my old age, or He may think fit to call me home; but while I live my wish will be to please you if I can benefit you, and my last prayers will be for your welfare."

"Oh, you must live on for many a day, and we must hear your story over and over again, till we know it by heart," cried Frank, about to go.

"Once for me to tell and once for you to hear would be enough, my dear lad," said Moggy, shaking her head.

"Good-bye, mother, good-bye," said Tom, his heart evidently touched by the poor old woman's condition.

"Fare thee well, my son, fare thee well. May Heaven prosper thee and guard thee on the perilous waters," answered Moggy, gazing intently at him as before. "So like thy countenance, and thy manners."

The rest of the party uttered their farewells, and leaving the hut, took their way down the mountain.

Chapter Eight.

Frank was the life of the family in the drawing-room, and Tom interested and astonished the inmates of the kitchen with the accounts he gave them of his own adventures and his young officer's exploits and gallant deeds. It is possible that some of his companions might have preferred hearing him sing a rollicking sea song, and seeing him dance a hornpipe, as most seamen are represented as doing on all possible occasions; but they soon found out that such was not Tom Holman's way. He could talk, though, and laugh, and be very merry at times, and never seemed unhappy; and Mary Jones, Mrs Morgan's old nurse, declared that he was the pleasantest, and nicest, and quietest, ay, and more than that, the best young man she had seen for many a day. Not that he was very young, for he was certainly over forty. Tom Holman was more than pleasant—he was an earnest, Christian seaman. Happily there are many such now-a-days, both in the Royal Navy and in the merchant service—men who are not ashamed of the Cross of Christ. Tom and Mrs Jones soon became fast friends, and it was through her that the way in which he and Frank first became intimate was known to Mrs Morgan and the rest of the family.

"You see, Mrs Jones," said Tom, as he sat with her in the housekeeper's room, "I was pretty well a castaway, without friends, without home, without any one to care for me, or show me the right course to sail on. I had got hold of some books, all about the rights of man, sneering at religion, and everything that was right, and noble, and holy; and in my ignorance I thought it all very fine, and had become a perfect infidel. All that sort of books writ by the devil's devices have brought countless beings to destruction—of body as well as of soul. Our ship was on the coast of Africa, employed in looking after slavers, to try and put a stop to the slave trade. I entered warmly into the work, for I thought that it was a cruel shame that men, because they had white skins, more power, and maybe, more sense, should be allowed to carry off their fellow-men and hold them in bondage. I was appointed as coxswain of the boat commanded by Mr Morgan. Often we used to be sent away in her for days together from the ship, to lie in wait for slavers. The officers on such occasions used to allow us to talk pretty freely to one another and to express our minds. One day I said something which showed Mr Morgan what was in my mind—how dark and ignorant it was. He questioned me further, and found that I was an infidel, that I had no belief in God or in goodness, and that I was unhappy. Some officers would have cared nothing for this, or just abused me, called me a fool, and let me alone; others, who called themselves religious, would have cast me off as a reprobate. But Mr Morgan, whom I always thought only a good-natured, merry young gentleman, did neither; but he stuck to me like a friend. Day after day, and night after night, he talked to me, and reasoned with me, and read to me out of the blessed Gospel, for he never was without the Book of Life in all our expedition. (See Note 1.) Whenever he could get me alone he pleaded earnestly with me, as a friend, nay, as affectionately as a brother. In spite of myself, he made me listen to him, and I learned to love and respect him, even when I thought myself far wiser than he was. He persevered. I began to see how vile I was, how unlike a pure and holy God; and then he showed me the only way by which I could become fit to dwell with God. It seemed so plain, so simple, so beautiful, so unlike any idea man could conceive, that I, as it were, sprang to it, just as a drowning man springs to a rock, and clutching it, lifts himself up clear of the tangled weeds which are dragging him to destruction. From that moment I became a changed man, and gained a peace and happiness of which I knew nothing before."

"Dr Morgan's regards, and he hopes you'll step into the dining-room, Mr Holman," said the parlour-maid, opening the door.

Tom was soon seated among the family circle, his manner showing that he was perfectly at his ease without the slightest show of presumption.

"Tom, they want to hear about our adventures, and I've told them that I must have you present to confirm my account, lest they should suppose I am romancing," said Frank, as Tom entered.

"They wouldn't think that, Mr Morgan," answered Tom. "But, however, I'll take the helm for a spell if you get out of your right course."

"I don't doubt you, old shipmate," said Frank. "But before I get under weigh with my yarn I want you to give them a few pages out of your log before you and I sailed together."

Tom guessed what this request meant. "Well, sir, if your honourable father and mother and you wish it, I'll tell you all I know about myself. For what I know to the contrary, I was born at sea. My first recollections were of a fearful storm on the ocean. We were tossing about in a boat. One of them, whom I for a long time afterwards thought was my father, had charge of me. He was a kind-hearted man, and looked after me most carefully. He went by the name of Jack Johnson, but sailors often change their names, especially if they have deserted, or have done anything for which they think that they may be punished. He always called me Tom, and I didn't know that I had any other name till he told me that my name was Holman, that he had known my father, who was a very respectable man, who, with my mother, and many other people, had been lost at sea. He said that he had saved me, and that we, with a few others, were the only people who had escaped from the wreck. We had been picked up by a ship outward bound round the Horn. Two of the men died, the rest entered on board the whaler, and as the captain could not well pitch me overboard he was obliged to take me; for indeed Jack, who was the best seaman of the lot, refused to do duty unless I was put on the ship's books for rations. It was a rough school for a child, but I throve in it, and learned many things, though some of them I had better not have learned. The captain seemed a stern and morose man, and for many months he took no notice of me; but one day as I was trying to climb up the rattlins of the lower shrouds I fell to the deck. He ran to me, lifted me up, and carrying me to his cabin, placed me on his own bed, and with an anxious countenance examined me all over to find where I was hurt. He rubbed my temples and hands, and Jack, who followed him into the cabin, said he looked quite pleased when I came to again. I was some weeks recovering, and he watched over me all the time with as much care as if I had been his own child.

"'Ah! the man's heart is in the right place, and I'd sooner sail with him than with many another softer-spoken gentleman I've fallen in with,' remarked Jack one day after I had recovered.

"We heard from one of the crew, who had before sailed with the captain, that he had a little son of his own killed from falling on deck, and this it was which made him take to me."

"Yes, God has implanted right and good feelings in the bosoms of all His creatures," observed the Doctor. "But when they are neglected, and sin is allowed to get the better of them, they are destroyed. None of our hearts are in their right place, as the saying is. They are all by nature prone to ill. The same man who was doing you the kindness might in other ways have been grievously offending God."

"Ay, sir, it might have been; but it would not become me to find fault with one who had rendered me so great a service," said Tom. "After I was well, he used to have me into his cabin every day to teach me to read and write, and the little learning I ever had I gained from him. We had been out four years, and the ship had at last got a full cargo, and was on the point of returning home, when we fell in with another ship belonging to the same owners. The captain of her had died, and the first mate had been washed overboard, and so the supercargo invited our captain to take charge of her. As he had no wife nor children living at home, this he consented to do, and thus it happened that I remained out in the Pacific another four years. Tom for my sake went with him to the other ship. We were nearly full.

"'One more fish, and then hurrah for old England, lads,' sung out the captain, as three sperm whales were seen spouting from the masthead.

"All the boats were immediately lowered. Jack was in the captain's boat. Away they pulled from the ship in chase. Those sperm whales are sometimes dangerous creatures to hunt. We saw that the captain's boat was fast, that is to say, he had struck the whale. Away went the boat, towed at a great rate. Suddenly she stopped—the whale rose. The captain pulled in to strike another harpoon into her. The monster reared her powerful tail and struck the boat a blow which split her clean in two. We had not a boat left to go to our shipmates' assistance; the other boats were far away in other directions. The wind was light, but we were able to lay up towards the spot where the accident had occurred. We could at length see the wreck of the boat and two men clinging to her. I hoped that one might be Jack and the other the captain; for they were, I may well say, the only two people I cared for in the world, or who cared for me. Eagerly I looked out. 'It's Jem Rawlins and Peter Garvin,' I heard some one say. My heart sank within me. Jem and Peter were got on board. They were, of all the crew, those I had the least reason to like. They told us that the poor captain had got the line entangled round his leg, and had been drawn down when the whale sounded, and that Jack had been killed by a blow from her tail. It seemed wonderful that they themselves should have escaped, considering the fury with which the whale attacked the boat. Thus was the last link broken which, as it were, connected me with my lost relations, and I might say that I had not a friend in the world. All I knew about myself was that Jack had saved me from the wreck of a ship called the 'Dove,' which, with my name, 'Tom Holman,' he had tattooed on my arm. He had also put into a tin case the belt I had on and one or two other little articles, which tin case was in his chest. It was unanimously agreed on board that I should be his heir, so I succeeded to the chest, the chief article of value in which was the tin case. I took it out, and have ever since preserved it carefully, though with little hope of finding it of use. I had become very fond of reading, and had read all the books in the captain's cabin. There were not many of them, and there was not one which had religion in it, and I am very certain that there was not a Bible on board. I only knew that there was such a book from the captain, who had read it at home, and I heard him only a few days before his death regretting that he had not got one. I believe our ship was not worse than others, and to the best of my belief not one of the South Sea whalers we fell in with had a Bible on board. The crews, as a rule, were lawless reprobates, and the masters petty tyrants, who cared nothing for the men, provided they would work to get their ships full. We sailed for England by the way of Cape Horn. I wished to go there because I wished to see what sort of a country it was, and to enjoy the amusements of which I heard the men talking. We had a prosperous passage till we were in the latitude of the Falkland Islands, when we were caught in a heavy gale, and after knocking about for some time in thick weather, when no observation could be obtained, we found ourselves with breakers under our lee, and a rocky shore beyond. The masts were cut away and anchors let go, but to no purpose; the ship parting from her anchors was driven on the rocks. Nearly half the crew were washed away, and the rest of us succeeded in gaining the shore, soon after which the ship went to pieces, and all the cargo which we had toiled so hard to collect was returned to the sea from whence it was obtained. Very few provisions came on shore, but there was a fair supply of canvas and plenty of ropes. We at once therefore put up a tent for ourselves, and placed all our more valuable possessions under cover. With some spars which came on shore we formed a lofty flagstaff, on which we hoisted a flag, in the hope that it might be seen by some passing vessel. There were springs of good water near the shore, and as long as our provisions lasted we got on pretty well, but when they began to fail the men looked at each other and asked, 'What next?'

"'Oh, some ship must be passing soon, and will take us off,' cried out two or three, who were unwilling to be placed on reduced rations.

"'But suppose no ship does pass, lads, what will you do? I have to tell you that, with the greatest economy, our provisions will not last another ten days,' said the first mate, who was now captain. 'It is barren and sandy here, but maybe, if we push our way across the island, we may find a richer country, and some animals on which we may live.'

"Some agreed to the mate's proposal, others determined to remain on the sea-shore. I accompanied the mate. The provisions were equally divided, and those who remained said they would try and catch some fish, in case theirs ran short.

"'Try and catch them at once, then,' said the mate; 'don't wait till you are starving.'

"In our party was a man who had been in South America, and could use the lasso with dexterity. He and another man fitted two lines for the purpose, in the hope of finding some wild animals. The rest laughed at them, declaring that in an island where there was not a tree to be seen, and only some long tufts of grass, it was not likely that we should find anything but snakes and lizards. We had made good some ten miles or so, when we came upon a scene of desolation such as I have seldom elsewhere met with. Far as the eye could reach the surface of the ground was one black mass of cinders. The men looked at each other.

"'Little prospect of finding any animals hereabouts,' observed one of the men.

"'Not so sure of that,' said the mate, kicking up the ashes with his foot. Under them appeared some blades of green grass just springing up.

"'To my mind the fire has run across the island at this part, which seems to be somewhat narrow, for from the top of that rock I climbed I could make out the sea on either hand; and thus, you understand, it may have driven the animals, if there are any, over to the other parts beyond, where I hope we may find them.'

"'But how is it that the animals didn't run our way?' asked one of the men.

"'Because the country where we have been is barren and sandy, and they have gone to the opposite side, which is very different. To the best of my belief we shall find herds of wild cattle feeding on the other side if we bravely push on. Here goes, who'll follow?'

"Saying this, the mate walked on quickly into the sea of cinders. I ran after him, and the rest followed. The mate supposed that the fire had occurred only a short time before we reached the island, and had been put out by the storm which had driven us on shore, or rather by the rain which accompanied it. We had to sleep that night in the middle of the cinders, without a drop of water to drink. Some of the men grumbled, but the mate told them that they ought to be thankful, because there was no chance of our being burned, which there might be if we were sleeping in the long grass.

"'Ah, lads, every situation has its advantages, if we will but look for them,' he remarked; and I have often since thought of that saying of his.

"On we went, the mate leading, the men often unwilling to proceed till he uttered a few words of encouragement. At last the sun's rays, bursting out from between the clouds, fell on some green grass which clothed the side of a hill before us. It was a welcome sight; and still more welcome was the sight of a herd of cattle which appeared before us as we got clear of the burnt district. It was important not to frighten them. We advanced carefully, the two men with lassoes leading, hiding ourselves among rocks and bushes, and keeping to leeward of the herd. To our great satisfaction, the animals as they fed moved on towards us. Suddenly the men with the lassoes threw them round the neck of a cow, the nearest animal to us. We sprang forward, laying hold of the ends, one party hauling one way, one the other. In spite of all her violent struggles, we had her fast, and one of the men, rushing in, hamstrung her, and she was in our power. This capture raised our spirits, for we felt sure that we should never want food on the island, as we might catch the oxen in pitfalls if not with lassoes. The mate was asked how he came to suppose that there were cattle on the island.

"'Just because a shipmate, in whose word I could trust, told me he had seen them,' was the answer. 'What better reason for believing a thing would you require?'

"We camped where we were, and the South American showed us how to cut up the heifer and to dry the meat in the sun, so that we had as much pure meat as each of us could carry. As our companions had enough food for some days longer, the mate wished to see more of the island before returning. We saw several large herds of cattle, which fed on the long grass covering the face of the country, which was generally undulating. We were several days away, and as we caught sight of the flagstaff, we thought of the pleasure the supply of meat we had brought would afford our companions. We saw the tents, but no one came to meet us. We shouted, but there was no shout in return. We feared that they might be ill, or even dead. We reached the tent, but no one was within; we looked about, we could find no one. The mate was looking seaward. He pointed to the offing, where, sinking below the horizon, the white sail of a ship was seen. It was more than probable that our shipmates had gone in her, but whether with their own will or carried off by force we could not conjecture. Some of the men were very angry, but the mate observed that was wrong. Our shipmates, probably, could not help themselves. They might have supposed we should not return, and, if they had gone with their own will, might have been unable to leave any message for us. The mate was a truly charitable man, for he was anxious to put the best construction on the conduct of our shipmates. There, however, we were left, with a diminished party, with the possibility that another ship might not approach the coast for many months to come. The summer was drawing to a close. It had been somewhat damp and cold, and we expected that the winter would be proportionally severe.

"'We may get off, but we may possibly have to stay; and if we are wise, lads, we shall prepare for the worst,' said the mate; and telling the men what would be wanted, forthwith began the work he advised.

"We were to build a couple of huts, to cut and dry turf for fuel, and to kill some cattle and prepare the flesh; to hunt for vegetables or herbs, which might keep off scurvy, and to do various other things.

"'Example is better than precept, Tom, as you will find,' observed the mate to me. 'I never tell men to do what I am not ready to do myself. That's the reason they obey me so willingly.'

"I've ever since remembered the mate's words, and told them to Mr Morgan; and I am sure he never orders men to do what he is not ready to try and do himself if necessary. It was fortunate for all that the mate's advice was followed. Some comfortable huts were got up, and a store of provisions and fuel collected before the winter began. It set in with unusual seventy, and I believe that we should all have perished from cold, and damp, and snow, had we not been prepared, though I do not remember that the frost was hard at any time.

"Some of the men abused their companions for going away without them.

"'Let be,' said the mate; 'all's for the best. We don't know where they are now, but we do know that we are not badly off, with a house, clothing, food, and firing. These islands are not so much out of the way, but what we are certain to get off some day or other, and in the meantime we have no cause to complain. Let us rather be thankful, and rejoice that we are so well off.'

"I remembered those words of the mate afterwards. It is now my belief that the mate was a God-fearing man, but religion had been so unpopular among those with whom he had sailed, that he was afraid of declaring his opinions, and just went and hid his light under a bushel. What a world of good he might have done us all if he had spoken out manfully! As it was, all that precious time was lost. The mate did speak to me occasionally, but timidly, and I did not understand him. How should I? It was not till long afterwards, as Mr Morgan knows, that I became acquainted with Christianity. Before that I was as a heathen; I knew nothing of Christ, nothing of God. The winter passed away, the spring returned, and the summer drew on, and not a sail had been seen. All hands became anxious to get off, and from early dawn till nightfall the flag was kept flying, and one or more of the party were on the lookout from Flagstaff Hill. At length a sail hove in sight. Nearer and nearer she came. 'Would our flag be seen?' was now the question. The wind was off the shore, she tacked, she was beating up towards us. From her white canvas and the length of her yards she was pronounced to be a man-of-war corvette, and her ensign showed us that she was English. Some of the men declared that they would rather live the rest of their days on the island than go on board a man-of-war; but the mate told them that they were very foolish, and that if they did their duty they would be better treated than on board most merchantmen. I shared their fears, for I had heard all sorts of stones about the treatment of men on board men-of-war, which I have since found to be absurdly false. The end was that we all stood ready to receive the boat when she reached the beach. A lieutenant with a midshipman came in her. They were very much surprised to hear that we had been a whole year on shore, observing that we must have saved a good supply of provisions from the wreck. When the mate told them of the wild cattle, and that we could catch some, they begged us to do so, saying that the purser would purchase the meat from us for the ship's company. They accordingly returned on board, but soon came back with the butcher, and by the next day we had six or eight fine animals ready for them. The officer kindly gave us permission to carry off any of our property which could be stowed away on board. From the considerate treatment the men received, they all volunteered into the service, and I was rated as a ship's boy, and from that day to this have belonged to the Royal Navy of England. The mate was promised promotion if he would join.

"'At all events I do not wish to eat the bread of idleness,' was his answer. 'I'll do duty in any station to which I am appointed.'

"The corvette was bound round the Horn, so back again into the Pacific I went. We touched at many places in Chili and Peru, and then stood to the west to visit some of the many islands in those seas. I had been about a year on board when one day an object was seen from the mast-head, which was made out to be a boat.

"There was one man sitting up in her, but three others lay dead under the thwarts. The man was brought on board more dead than alive, and had it not been for the watchful care of our surgeon he could not have long survived. At first he was nothing but skin and bone, with sunken eyes and hollow cheeks, but when he got some flesh on him I recognised him as one of my shipmates who had deserted us on the Falkland Islands. He had not, it seemed, discovered any of us, and of course in two years I was so grown that he did not know me. So one day, sitting by him, I asked him how it was he came into the plight in which we found him. He told me many circumstances of which I was cognisant, and how the ship was wrecked on the Falklands, and how part of the people had gone off into the interior, and deserted those who wisely remained on the sea-shore. 'Never mind, they must have got their deserts, and perished,' he added; and then he told me a ship appearing the day after we left, they had all gone on board. They soon found that the crew had been guilty of some foul deed; the captain and mate had been killed, with some others, and the rest had determined to turn pirates. My shipmate was asked if he would do so. They swore if he did not that he must die. To save his life, he with the rest consented to join them. I will not repeat the account he gave of all the crimes which he and his companions had committed. He said that he had protested against them, and excused himself. From bad they went on to worse, and frequently quarrelling, murdered each other. The end was that this ship was cast away on a reef, one boat only escaping, and of the people in her, after she had been nearly a month drifting over the ocean, he alone survived. We who had been left alone on the Falklands had reason to be thankful that we had not gone off in the pirate ship. Had we done so, who among us could have said that we should have escaped the terrible fate which overtook our shipmates? From the time I learned the Lord's Prayer, there is no part I have repeated more earnestly than 'Lead us not into temptation.' My poor shipmate never completely recovered from the hardships to which he had been exposed; his mind, too, was always haunted with the dreadful scenes he had witnessed, and he often told me that he never could show his face in England, lest he should be recognised by those he had wronged. He died the day before we made the coast of England. The ship was paid off, but I found the naval service so much to my taste, and there was so little on shore to attract me, that I the next day joined another fitting out for the Indian station. After this, I visited in one ship or another most parts of the world. But I think, Doctor Morgan, you and your lady and the young gentlefolks will be getting tired, so I'll put off an account of my adventures till another evening. One thing I must say now, though. I looked upon it as a blessed day on which I joined the 'Rover,' where I met Mister Morgan, and yet there was a day which I have reason to call still more blessed, when we were off the coast of Africa."

" He was swimming towards me."

"Well, well, Tom. Don't talk of that now," said Frank. "I just did what every Christian man should do. I put the truth before you, and you believed it. I did not put myself to any inconvenience even to serve Tom, while he risked his life to save mine. That was after the 'Rover' had come home and been paid off, and we belonged to the 'Kestrel,' and were sent out to the Pacific. I had an idea before we went there that we were to find at all times calm seas and sunshine. I soon discovered my mistake. We were caught in a terrific gale when in the neighbourhood of coral islands and reefs. I had gone aloft to shorten sail, when the ship gave an unexpected lurch, and I was sent clean overboard. I felt that I must be lost, for the ship was driving away from me, and darkness was not far off, when I saw that some one had thrown a grating into the sea, and immediately afterwards a man leaped in after it. He was swimming towards me. There seemed a prospect of my being saved. Still, how the man who had thus nobly risked his life for my sake, and I could ever regain the ship, I could not tell. I struck out with all my strength to support myself, and prayed heartily. I soon recognised Tom Holman's voice, cheering me up. He clutched me by the collar, and aided by him I gained the grating. Two or three spars had been thrown in after it, and, getting hold of them we formed a raft which supported us both. By the time we were seated on it the ship was far away, and it seemed impossible that in the dangerous neighbourhood in which I knew that we were, the captain would venture to return on the mere chance of finding us, should we indeed be alive. Our prospect outwardly was gloomy indeed, though we kept up hope. I was sorry when I thought that we should be lost; that Tom had, as I fancied, thrown away his life for my sake. However, we will not talk of that now. We were drifting, that was certain, and might drift on shore, or we might be driven against a reef, when we must be lost. It was now night, though there was light enough to distinguish the dark white-crested seas rising up around us, and the inky sky overhead. Still we knew that there was the Eye of Love looking down on us through that inky sky, and that though the rest of the world was shut out from us, we were not shut out from Him, without whose knowledge not a sparrow falls to the ground. I say this to you, dear father and mother, because I wish to show my brothers and sisters the effect of your teaching. I wished to live, but I was prepared to die. The water was warm, and as we had had supper just before I fell overboard we were not hungry, so that our physical sufferings were as yet not great. Hour after hour passed by; the raft drove on before the wind and sea. We supposed that it must be near dawn, for it seemed as if we had been two whole nights on the raft, when we both heard the sound of breakers. Our fate would soon thus be decided. As far as we were able, we gazed around when we reached the summit of a sea. There were the breakers; we could see the white foam flying up like a vast waterspout against the leaden sky. We were passing it though, not driving against it. A current was sweeping us on. The dawn broke. As the light increased our eyes fell on a grove of cocoa-nut trees, rising it seemed directly out of the water. The current was driving us near them. We sat up and eagerly watched the shore; we had of ourselves no means of forcing on the raft a point towards it, or in any degree faster than we were going. Had we been driven directly towards it, on the weather side, which, in our eagerness, we might have wished, we should probably have been dashed to pieces; but the current took us round to the lee side, and finally drifted us into a little bay where we safely got on shore. You already know how we lived luxuriously on cocoa-nuts and shell-fish, and about the clear fountain which rushed up out of the rock in the centre of our island, and how our ship came back after some weeks to water at that very fountain, and found us safe and well; and so I will bring my yarn to an end."

"We cannot be too thankful that you were preserved, my dear boy, when we hear of the terrific dangers to which you and your brave friend were exposed," exclaimed Dr Morgan. "I will not now speak of our debt to him, never properly to be repaid, but I would point out to you all, my children (what struck me as Frank was speaking), how like the way in which he and Tom were preserved, is that in which God deals with His people who put their trust in Him. We are in an ocean of troubles, with darkness around us. We dimly discern breakers rising up on one side, breakers ahead. We can do nothing to help ourselves, except pray on and trust in Him. We see at length a haven of safety before us. Our eagerness gets the better of our faith, but the current of His mercy drifts round and away from what is really a peril, and we are carried on into calm waters, and find shelter and rest from danger and trouble."

Note 1. The author has a dear friend, a naval officer, who was, as is here described, the instrument of bringing some of his shipmates to a knowledge and acceptance of the truth; one especially, from being an infidel, became a faithful follower of Christ. His bones lie sepulchred under the eternal snows of the Arctic pole. How consolatory to believe, that amid the fearful sufferings that gallant band was called on to endure, he, with many others—it may be all—were supported by faith and hope to the last. We say all, for we cannot say what influence he and other Christian men may have exerted over their companions during the long, long years they passed in those Arctic regions ere they perished.

Chapter Nine.

Several circumstances had prevented the young Morgans from paying a sufficiently long visit to Old Moggy to enable her to give them her promised history. Jenny reported that she was better in mind and body than she had ever known her, and as the time for Frank and Tom's departure was drawing near, the whole party resolved to go up to hear her tale. They did not fail to carry a few little luxuries which were likely to please her. They found her as usual, seated before her fire, for even in the summer she seemed to enjoy its warmth, on that bleak hill's side. What with chairs, benches, and stools, a log of wood, a pile of turf, and a boulder which Charley rolled in, all found seats. Anna had to exercise a little diplomacy to induce Moggy to begin before so formidable an audience. The poor creature was inclined to chide Tom for not having come up oftener to see her, when she discovered that he was going away.

"I took a liking to your face and your manner my son, from the first minute my eyes fell on you; and it would have been a slight thing for ye to have come up and cheered the old woman's well-nigh withered heart," she observed, in a more testy tone than she was accustomed to use.

"Well, mother, don't blame me," answered Tom. "Many's the time I've come round this way, but feared to intrude, or I would have come in, and I'll not now miss the chance another time."

This promise seemed to satisfy Moggy, and after a little hesitation she began.

"Once I was blithe and gay as any of you dear young people. I had a home, and parents, and sisters. There were three of us, as pretty and as merry as any to be found in the country around. We merrily grew up into happy maidens, as merry as could be found, and the glass told us, even if others had been silent, that we were as pretty too. We sang and laughed from morn till night, and, alack, were somewhat thoughtless too; but we were not idle. Our parents had a farm, and we helped our mother in the dairy, and there was plenty of work for us. It was a pleasant life. We were up with the lark and to bed in summer with the sun, and in winter we sat by the fire when the cows were housed and the milk was set in the pans, and all our out-door work was done, and knitted or spun, or plied our needles, and chatted and sung; and guests came in, and some of them came to woo; and we thought not of the morrow, and taught ourselves to believe that the pleasant life we led would never have an end. Ah! we were foolish—like the foolish virgins who had no oil for their lamps, as all are foolish who think only of the present, and prepare not for the future. Bad times were in store for us, such as all farmers must be ready to encounter. Storms injured the crops, and disease attacked our cattle; a fire broke out in the farm buildings; and the end was that father had to throw up the farm, to sell his remaining stock, and to go forth almost penniless into the world. Barely enough remained to pay our passage to America. I was about to go with the rest of my family, when one I had loved right well, an honest, steady youth, entreated me to remain. He might soon have enough to wed. He had a sick mother whom he could not leave, or he would have gone with us. If I went we might never meet again. I consented to remain, so that I could obtain service in which to support myself. A kind, good mistress engaged me. She was more than kind, she was wise; not worldly wise, but her wisdom was from above. She taught me that wisdom. By her means my eyes were opened to things about which I before knew nothing. I saw that God had dealt mercifully with me; that what I thought was a misfortune was a blessing. I was thus led out of darkness into light. I was happy, with a new happiness of which I before knew nothing. My intended husband enjoyed it likewise; we both embraced the truth—my only sorrow being that those who had gone away knew nothing of it. Thomas lived at a distance, but whenever he could he came over to see me. My kind, good mistress often spoke to him, and approved of my choice. Time wore on. We waited to hear of those who had crossed the sea. Sad tidings came at length. My mother had died on the voyage. My father, heart-broken, and my sisters had landed and found a home, but they missed her who had been their guide and their friend; and they wanted me to go out and join them, and some cousins who lived a few miles off from where I was at service, and Thomas also, if he would marry me. I told my kind mistress.

"'If Thomas loves you, and will take you to that foreign land, I will not say you nay,' was her reply.

"She gave me leave to go and deliver the message to my cousins, charging me soon to return. My cousins were not averse to my sister's proposal, and talked with pleasure of the many kindred who would meet in that far-off settlement, for far off it seemed to them. On my return I found the front door of my mistress's house closed. I went round and gained an entrance through a window at the back. What was my horror to find her bathed in blood, fallen from the arm-chair in which she sat before the fire. I kneeled down to examine where she had been hurt, and was about to raise her up when the door was burst open; some men rushed in; I was seized. No one aided my dear mistress. A surgeon at length came. He pronounced her dead. These cruel men had allowed her to die unaided. I was accused of being her murderess. My horror, my indignation, at the way she had been treated, my grief, my agitation, impressed them with the conviction that I was guilty of the foul crime which had been committed; for murdered she had been, of that there was no doubt. Branded as a murderess I was borne off to prison. Many thought me guilty. It was cruelly said that I was found red-handed by the side of my victim. But even in prison I sought support, and obtained it whence alone it was to be afforded. As King David, I could say, 'I have washed my hands in innocency. I cried unto the Lord and He heard me.' Oh, my young friends, keep innocency. Do what is right in the sight of the Lord, and never need you fear what man can do unto you. There was one, however, on earth who knew me to be innocent—my Thomas. He obtained leave to visit me in prison, obtained the best legal aid by the sacrifice of his savings, and the evidence against me broke completely down. I was acquitted. I scarcely knew how, or what occurred. I entreated Thomas to let me become his wife, that I might repay him by devoting my life to his service. We married; we were happy; and by watchful care I was enabled to make his wages go farther than before his marriage. More than a year had passed away; we had a child born, a son. We believed that he would prove a blessing to us. Some few more years had fled by. Again and again my sisters urged that we would go out to join them. At length they were both about to marry, and our father would be left alone. Thomas agreed to go. I thought with delight of showing my young son to my father, of assisting and supporting him in his old age, and more than all, of imparting to him those blessed truths which I myself had found such a comfort to my soul. We sailed in as fine a ship as ever put to sea, with many others about to seek their fortunes in the New World; but scarcely had we left the shores of England a hundred leagues astern than we encountered a fearful gale, which washed away the bulwarks and some of our boats, strained the hull, and shattered our masts and spars. It was but the beginning of disasters. But, dear young people, I cannot dwell on that most grievous period of my existence. The storm had injured our provisions. After the storm came a calm, more dreadful than the storm; our water began to run short. Did any of you ever feel the pangs of thirst? Day after day our shattered bark lay rolling on the burning ocean. There was the constant gush of water to tantalise us, for by undiscovered leaks the sea had found an entrance, and in every watch the pumps were kept at work. We were thankful when a breeze came, and once more the ship moved across the ocean; but the breeze increased into a gale more fearful than the first. On, on we drove; the leaks again increased. Day and night the men were kept toiling at the pumps; my husband worked like the rest. In vain, in vain; they could work no longer; the water was gaining on us; the raging seas were washing over our decks. The strength of the men was exhausted. Some of the women offered to try and work the pumps. The night was coming on. I resolved to labour, that I might aid to save my husband's life, our boy's, my own.

"My boy had clung to me. I gave him, so I thought, to his father, to watch over, while I laboured like the rest. Would you hear what occurred? My heart has grown into stone, or I could not bear to tell it. The raging seas broke more and more frequently over the ship. The dreadful cry arose, 'The ship is sinking, the ship is sinking!' I flew towards my husband—my child was not with him. He had not received him from me. Frantically I rushed along the deck; it was with no hope of safety, but to die with my boy in my arms. Once more I was approaching my husband; a flash of lightning revealed him to me at the moment that a vast sea came sweeping down on the ship. It seized him in its cruel embrace, and bore him far, far away, with many other helpless, shrieking beings. Thankfully would I have followed, but I sought my boy. In vain, in vain! I felt myself seized by a strong arm, and lifted into a boat. I lost all consciousness for the next instant, it seemed. I found the boat floating alone amid the tumultuous waves. My husband and my boy were gone. They said there were other boats, and that some might have been saved in them. I know not if any were saved. Neither my husband nor our child did I ever again see; the cold, cruel waves had claimed them. For many days we lay tossed about on the foaming waters. We were more dead than alive when a sail appeared in sight. How I lived I know not; it was, I believe, because all my feelings were dead. I felt nothing, thought of nothing; I was in a dream, a cold, heavy weight lay on my heart and brain. I knew not what was going on; the past was a blank, the future was darkness. We were lifted on board — carefully tended. The ship was bound, with settlers, to the same port to which I was going. Those who had been saved with me told my story. Some of the passengers were going to the far-off West, to the very spot where my father and sisters had settled. Their hearts were touched with compassion by my misfortunes, and they bore me with them. Truly they were followers of the good Samaritan. Day after day we journeyed on towards the setting sun. At length we reached my father's house; he and my sisters scarcely knew me, so great was the havoc grief had wrought. Kind and gentle treatment by degrees thawed my long frozen faculties, and I began to take an interest in the affairs of the farm. In that region the native tribes, the red men of the prairie, were fierce and warlike, and often were engaged in deadly contests with the whites. Years—many years, passed by, during which our people enjoyed peace. A storm, however, was brewing, to burst with fury on our heads. It came; in the dead of night the dreadful war-whoop of the red men was heard. On every side arose those horrid cries. Our village was surrounded; young and old, men and maidens, were ruthlessly murdered. My old father and sisters were among the first slain. Some few bravely made a stand. They fought their way out through the savages. I felt my arm seized by some friendly hand, and was borne on amid them. Armed friends came to our assistance, and the savages were driven back through the smoking ruins of our home. All, all were gone; relatives, friends, and property. Those who had accompanied me to the country, all, all were gone. I was among strangers; they pitied me, but pity cannot last long in the human breast. There is only One whose tender pity never wanes; and it is only that human pity which arises from love of Him which can stand all tests, and can endure for ever. I was left alone, alone in that far-off land. My reason gave way. An idea had seized me—it was to visit that mighty ocean beneath which slept my husband and my child. I wandered on. I know not how I found my way, often through vast solitudes where foot of man but rarely trod, till I reached the more settled states. Food and shelter were rarely denied to the poor mad woman, though of the roughest sort. At length I reached the eastern cities; scant was the charity I found within them, I gained the sea-coast; I gazed upon the ocean, with its majestic billows rolling up from the far-off east. They seemed to me like mighty monuments raised to the memory of those who slept beneath. For many years I had lived on that wild sea waste, when I was seized and carried to a prison. I demanded to know my crime. I heard myself branded as a pauper lunatic, and was placed on board a ship to be returned to my native land. Sad, sad was my heart. I had many companions in my misery—helpless beings whom the strong new world would not receive. We were placed on shore to starve, or live as best we could. I wandered on towards the spot where long, long years before, I had lived a happy maiden. No one knew me; I was branded as a witch, and fled away. Should I go to the relatives of my husband? Thomas had spoken of them as kind and charitable. I reached the village; every one looked at me with suspicion as a vagrant. Well they might, for a vagrant I was, poor, wretched, and despised. I had been there in my happy days with Thomas; but the place itself looked strange. I inquired for his father, Farmer Holman. 'Dead many a year ago; all the rest gone away; never held up his head since his son went off with that jade who murdered her mistress.' Such was the answer I received. The words fell like molten lead upon my brain. I fled away. I wandered on, not knowing whither I was going, till I reached these sheltering walls on the mountain-side."

Tom had been greatly agitated on hearing the name of Holman. Frank and Anna had exchanged surprised glances with each other.

"Dame, do you remember the name of Jack Johnson on board the ship which foundered with so many on board?" asked Tom.

"Ay, that I do. He was one who took a great fancy to my precious boy," answered Moggy, gazing earnestly at Tom.

"It is strange, mother, but such was the name of a kind seaman who for many years acted as a second father to me; and still stranger, that he always called me Tom Holman," exclaimed Tom, as he sat himself down on the stool at her feet, and drawing a tin case from his pocket, took from it a variety of small articles, which he placed in her lap.

She gazed at them with a fixed, earnest look for some moments, and then, stretching out her arms, she exclaimed, "Come to me, my son, my boy—long lost, now found! I cried unto the Lord, and He heard me out of my deep distress. You bear your father's name, you have your father's looks. Wonderful are the ways of the Lord. The Lord giveth and the Lord taketh away. The Lord hath restored me tenfold into my bosom. Blessed be the Name of the Lord!"

Tom threw his arms round the old woman, and sobbed like a child.

"Mother, mother, I have found you, I have found you!" he cried out, as he kissed her withered cheek.

What mattered it to him that she was aged and infirm, poor and despised? She was his mother, of whom he had dreamed in his youth whom he had always longed to find. He would now devote himself to cherish and support her, and cheer her few remaining days on earth.

"My dear children," said Dr Morgan, who had entered soon after Moggy had begun her history, "let us learn, from what we have heard, never to cease to put our whole trust and confidence in God.

Whatever happens, let us go on praying to God and trusting in God, for let us be assured that He always careth for us."

The End.

Copyright © 2021 Esprios Digital Publishing. All Rights Reserved.

Lightning Source UK Ltd.
Milton Keynes UK
UKHW040631060921
390110UK00001B/44